Classic Literature

Macbeth

by

William Shakespeare

retold by
Jerry Stemach
and
Gail Portnuff Venable

Don Johnston Incorporated
Volo, Illinois

Edited by:

Jerry Stemach, MS, CCC-SLP
AAC Specialist, Adaptive Technology Center, Sonoma County, California

Gail Portnuff Venable, MS, CCC-SLP
Speech-Language Pathologist, Scottish Rite Center for Childhood Language Disorders, San Francisco, California

Dorothy Tyack, MA
Learning Disabilities Specialist, Scottish Rite Center for Childhood Language Disorders, San Francisco, California

Consultant:
Ted S. Hasselbring, PhD
Professor of Special Education, Vanderbilt University, Nashville, TN

Cover Design and Illustration: Karyl Shields and Bob Stotts

Interior Illustrations: Bob Stotts

Copyright © 2000 Start-to-Finish Publishing. All rights reserved.

The Don Johnston logo and Start-to-Finish are trademarks of Don Johnston Incorporated. All rights reserved.

Published by:

Don Johnston Incorporated
26799 West Commerce Drive
Volo, IL 60073

Printed in the U.S.A. No part of this publication may be reproduced, stored in a retrieval system or transmitted in any form or by any means electronic, mechanical photocopying recording, or otherwise.

International Standard Book Number
ISBN 1-58702-318-0

Contents

Part 1
News from the War 5

Part 2
The Witches 14

Part 3
The Plan 24

Part 4
The Murder 35

Part 5
The Dream Comes True 43

Part 6
The Ghost 52

Part 7
Macbeth and the Witches 61

Part 8
Smoke and Blood 69

Part 9
The Forest Moves 79

Part 10
Macbeth Meets the Thane of Fife 89

A Note from the Start-to-Finish Editors

Part 1

News from the War

Outside the royal army camp, a soldier was shouting, "Where is King Duncan! Take me to the King! I have news about the war!"

King Duncan was the King of Scotland. He was a good king, and most of the people in Scotland loved him. The King had other men who helped him rule the country. These men were called Lords or Thanes. One of them was the Thane of Cawdor. Cawdor had become a traitor. He was using his own army to fight a war against the King.

Now, one of King Duncan's soldiers had come back from the war. He was badly hurt, but he wanted to report to the King about the battles. Quickly, the soldier was brought to King Duncan.

"Tell us the news!" cried the King. "How are my generals doing?"

The soldier wiped away the blood and sweat from his face. "At first, it was easy," he said.

"We found Cawdor's army in a small valley. General Macbeth charged down into the valley from the left side with some of our men. General Banquo and General Macduff charged down from the right side with the rest of our soldiers. Cawdor's army got scared and ran away," said the soldier. "Then Macbeth attacked one of the leaders and cut off his head. He put the head on a post to frighten the soldiers, and it worked! The soldiers ran away in horror."

"Excellent," said King Duncan. "Macbeth is bold and clever."

"Yes," replied the soldier. "We thought that the war was over. But later that day, Cawdor arrived with many more soldiers. These new soldiers came from Norway."

The King looked worried. "What happened next?" he asked. "Were Macbeth and Banquo afraid?"

"No, sir," said the soldier. "Is a lion afraid of a rabbit? Is an eagle afraid of a sparrow? General Macbeth was not afraid! Macbeth led the attack. He fought like a madman. He swung his sword so hard that none of Cawdor's soldiers could stop him. General Banquo and General Macduff and the rest of the army followed Macbeth," he continued. "We attacked and killed every enemy soldier that we could find. Now we have won the war and we have captured Cawdor."

The King turned to two of his men and said, "Cawdor must die for his crimes against me. Go and kill him," said the King. "When Cawdor is dead, tell Macbeth that he is the new Thane of Cawdor."

King Duncan told his servants to get ready for a trip. Then he went to find his two sons, Malcolm and Donalbain.

The King told his sons, "Tomorrow we shall ride to the city of Inverness to General Macbeth's castle. There we shall have a great celebration for Macbeth and Banquo and Macduff because they are the bravest generals in my kingdom."

Part 2

The Witches

After the battle with Cawdor was over, Macbeth and Banquo rode their horses down, out of the mountains. The sky was getting dark, and the two men could see storm clouds ahead.

Suddenly, there was a flash of lightning. Thunder boomed, and the horses jumped.

As the two men turned their horses back onto the road, they saw three shapes standing in the road.

"Are they animals or men?" Macbeth asked Banquo.

"I don't know," replied Banquo. "Are they dead or alive?"

Lightning flashed again and lit up the road.

This time, Macbeth could see that the shapes were not animals or men. The shapes seemed to be three old women. Their clothes were dirty rags. Their long, gray hair blew about their faces, and their backs were bent.

Macbeth was a brave man, but these women scared him. They stared at him with yellow eyes.

The old women pointed their long, bony fingers at Macbeth and Banquo, but they did not speak. Macbeth thought that he could see hair growing on their wrinkled faces.

"Witches!" Banquo thought to himself.

"Who are you?" cried Macbeth to the women. "Speak!"

The first witch spoke. "All hail to you, Macbeth!" she said.

Macbeth was surprised that they knew his name.

"All hail to Macbeth, the Thane of Cawdor!" said the second witch.

"Why do you say this to me?" asked Macbeth. "I am not the Thane of Cawdor!"

Then the third witch spoke. "You are the Thane of Cawdor today. You are the King of Scotland tomorrow!" she said.

Then the first witch spoke to Banquo. "And you, Banquo. You will not be king," she said. "But you will be the father of kings!" And with those words, the three witches disappeared.

Banquo was the first one to speak. "Where did they go?" he asked Macbeth. "Were they really here, or are we going insane?"

A few minutes later, the King's messengers arrived on horseback. "Good evening," said the first messenger. "We bring greetings and good news from King Duncan."

"What news?" asked Macbeth.

"Good sir," said the messenger to Macbeth. "The King has heard about your brave deeds in the war.

Classic Literature

The Thane of Cawdor has been put to death, and the King wants you to take his place. *You* are the Thane of Cawdor now."

Next, the second messenger spoke. "Tomorrow, King Duncan and his sons, Malcolm and Donalbain, will ride to your castle at Inverness," he said. "They wish to thank you for winning the war."

Then, the two messengers turned their horses around and rode back to the King's castle.

Macbeth spoke to Banquo. "I am the Thane of Cawdor!" he said. "The witches were right! Perhaps your children shall be kings!"

These events upset Banquo. He grabbed Macbeth by the arm. "Forget about the witches," said Banquo. "They say foolish things." And he rode off down the path alone.

But Macbeth could not forget about the witches. He kept seeing a picture in his mind. In this picture, he was sitting on a throne and wearing a crown. In this picture, Macbeth was the King of Scotland.

Part 3

The Plan

Lady Macbeth stood alone in her castle. She was reading a letter from her husband. In his letter, Macbeth told his wife about the witches. "The witches saw the future," he had written. "And they said that I would be King."

Lady Macbeth held the letter tightly in her hands. She was a greedy woman, and she wanted very much to be the Queen. "Oh, Macbeth!" she said to herself. "I know what you must do to become King. But I am afraid that you are not evil enough to do it."

As she was thinking these wicked thoughts, a messenger arrived from King Duncan. He bowed his head to Lady Macbeth. "King Duncan will soon be here," he said. "He will spend the night in your castle. The King wishes to celebrate the victory with you and Macbeth." Then the messenger turned and rode away.

Lady Macbeth was amazed. "This is our chance!" she said to herself. "Of course we must murder King Duncan now. Tonight he will ride right into my trap."

Just then, Macbeth arrived. He jumped down from his horse and went inside to find his wife. "King Duncan and his sons will be here tonight," he said to her.

"I know," whispered Lady Macbeth. "And they must never leave this castle alive." Lady Macbeth put her hands on his shoulders. "I have a plan," she said. "You must act as if you love the king, but secretly you will be like a snake that is waiting to attack him."

Macbeth pulled away from his wife. "No, I cannot do this," he replied. "The King has just made me Thane of Cawdor. I cannot hurt him," he said.

"Oh, my husband!" said Lady Macbeth. "You must want to be King, or you would not have told me about the witches. Where is your courage? Are you so weak that you just make up dreams and then let the dreams die? I have a plan," she said again. "Just leave everything to me."

That evening, King Duncan and his sons, Malcolm and Donalbain, arrived at the castle with Banquo and Banquo's son, Fleance. The King's two guards followed behind them. Macbeth and his wife greeted the King. "We are pleased that you are here, sir," said Lady Macbeth. "Thank you for coming."

The King smiled at Lady Macbeth. "*I* have come to thank *you*," he said. "You have acted bravely in the war, Macbeth. Let us celebrate our victory!"

That night, Lady Macbeth held a feast for the King and the other guests. She kept telling the servants to pour more and more wine. She wanted to get everyone drunk so that they would sleep soundly. Lady Macbeth poured wine into her own cup, too, but she only pretended to drink it. She wanted to be able to think clearly. After three hours, all the guests were drunk. One by one, they staggered off to bed.

Part 3   Macbeth   **31**

Macbeth had left the feast early. He could not stop thinking about the murder, so he could not bear to be with the King. Lady Macbeth found her husband alone in the courtyard.

"I cannot do this evil deed," said Macbeth to his wife. "Duncan is my King! I have been his loyal friend. It is my job to protect him from his enemies."

But Lady Macbeth would not give up. "Don't be a fool!" she said. "Remember what the witches said! 'Today, you are Thane of Cawdor and tomorrow you will be King of Scotland!'"

Macbeth did not want to look at his wife, but she forced him to pay attention.

She spoke again. "The King and his guards are drunk," she told Macbeth.

"When I am sure that they are all asleep, I will take the daggers from the guards," said Lady Macbeth. "I will leave the daggers on Duncan's bed. When everything is ready, I will ring my bell."

Part 4

The Murder

At midnight, Banquo came out into the courtyard. He saw Macbeth and spoke to him. "I'm afraid to go to sleep," Banquo whispered. "Last night, I dreamed about the three witches. Now I believe that they have told you the truth."

Macbeth looked at Banquo and said, "I don't think about the witches any more." But Macbeth was lying.

After Banquo left him, Macbeth became more and more upset. He walked nervously back and forth across the courtyard.

Then, suddenly, he stopped moving. Macbeth was frozen in fear. He thought that he could see a dagger floating in the air in front of him. Now it seemed that the dagger was covered with blood! Macbeth reached out his hand to see if the dagger was real. At that moment, he heard the bell ring, and he knew that he could not wait any longer. Silently, he crept into the bedroom where Duncan was sleeping.

The light from the moon was shining into the room. The daggers were waiting for him.

Macbeth could see that the King and his two guards were sound asleep. He wanted to run away. His head felt hot and his hands were shaking. He didn't know what he was doing. Now he was standing over the sleeping King. He could feel something warm on his fingers. He looked down and saw blood. He saw that he was holding a dagger in each hand. Blood was dripping onto his hands. King Duncan was dead! The bed sheet that covered him was wet and red. Macbeth could smell the blood.

One of the guards woke up and called out, and then he went back to sleep. Had the guard seen Macbeth? Macbeth was not sure. The other guard moaned.

Macbeth staggered back out of the room. "I have done the deed," he whispered to his wife. "But what will happen to me now if everyone finds out that I have killed the king?"

"We will blame this murder on those two guards in there," she explained. "We will say that they got drunk and they did not know what they were doing.

40 Classic Literature

But first you must go back in there and put these bloody daggers in their hands," she said.

Macbeth just stood there and stared at his wife. He did not move.

Lady Macbeth grabbed the daggers from her husband and rushed into the bedroom herself. Now her hands were bloody, also. The guards were asleep again, so she wiped some of the blood on their clothes. Then she put the daggers in their hands and rushed out of the room.

Macbeth was still standing in the hallway when she returned. She pulled at his sleeve. "Come away from here," she said. "A little water will wash away this murder from our hands!"

Macbeth was still washing the blood from his hands when he heard a loud banging on the door of the castle. He shivered with terror. BANG! BANG! BANG! "Open the door!" someone shouted from outside. "I have a meeting with the King!"

Part 5

The Dream Comes True

"Someone is at the door!" cried Lady Macbeth to her husband when she heard the loud banging. "Go and open it! Remember that you have nothing to be afraid of," she said. "Pretend that we have been sleeping."

Macbeth walked quickly to the castle door and opened it. There was General Macduff, the Thane of Fife.

"Macduff, my friend," said Macbeth. "Good morning to you. Come in."

"The King asked me to meet with him this morning," said Macduff. "But I am late. Is he here?"

"Yes," said Macbeth. "He should be awake by now. Come with me. I will take you to his room."

Macbeth went down a hallway and opened the bedroom door. Then he waited while Macduff went in. Macbeth did not have to wait long before he heard Macduff scream from inside the room. Macduff began to shout, "Murderers! Traitors! The King has been murdered by traitors." Everyone in the castle came running into the hallway.

Lady Macbeth looked nervously at her husband. Banquo was watching both of them. "What has happened?" asked Lady Macbeth.

"Our King has been murdered by someone in this castle!" shouted Macduff.

"But everyone in this castle is a loyal citizen of Scotland," replied Lady Macbeth.

"No!" cried Macduff. "Someone among us is *not* a loyal citizen. Someone here is a traitor against Scotland! Go and see for yourself, Macbeth."

Macbeth went to Duncan's room. When he returned, he moaned, "The great and good king is dead. What can this mean? The king's own guards must have done this deed, since the bloody daggers are in their hands. But they will never murder anyone again," said Macbeth.

"When I saw the dead king, I was so angry that I could not control myself," said Macbeth. "I killed the guards with their own daggers."

"Where are Malcolm and Donalbain?" asked Macduff. "Has anyone told them that their father has been murdered?"

"Yes, sir," said a soldier. "And both of them have left the castle. Malcolm is on his way to England, and Donalbain has left for Ireland. They were afraid that their lives were also in danger here," he said.

"Then who shall be King of Scotland?" asked Lady Macbeth.

"The crown belongs to the Thane of Cawdor," replied Macduff. "The crown belongs to Macbeth."

Banquo remembered what the three witches had said to Macbeth. "Macbeth is now the King," said Banquo to himself. "But I'm afraid that he is the one who has killed Duncan."

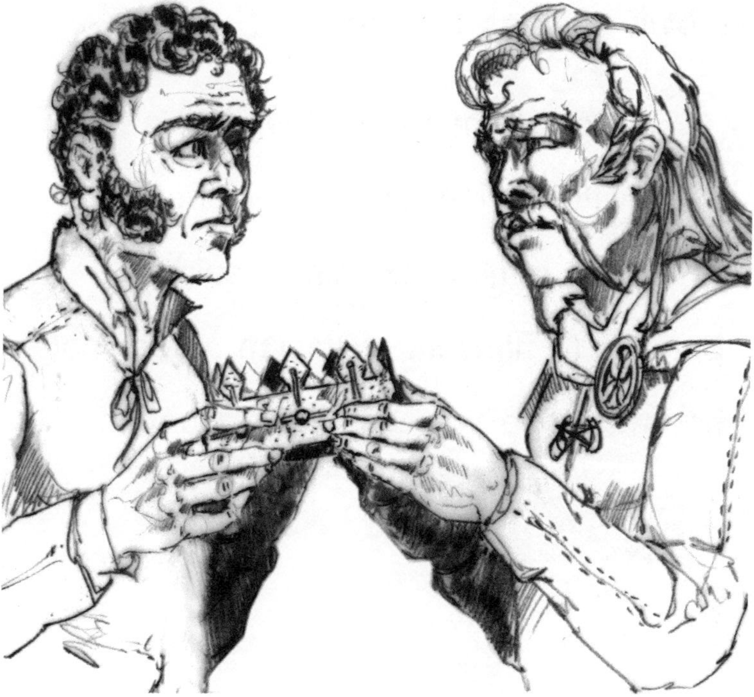

Then Banquo remembered what the witches had said to him. They had told him that he would be the father of kings. This gave Banquo a new worry. "Perhaps my son, Fleance, is not safe here either," he said. "Perhaps Macbeth will be jealous of him. Macbeth may kill him."

Part 6

The Ghost

The people of Scotland were saddened by the news of King Duncan's death. Macbeth and his wife were now living in the royal castle as the new King and Queen. But the Lords and Thanes and citizens of Scotland were not happy. Macbeth's dream of being King began to feel more like a nightmare.

"I am the King for now," Macbeth told his wife. "But Banquo's son, Fleance, will soon be King himself."

"Why do you say that?" asked Lady Macbeth.

"The witches told us," said Macbeth. "They said that Banquo would be the father of kings."

"What can you do?" asked the Queen.

"There is only one thing that I can do," replied Macbeth. "I must order my men to kill Banquo and Fleance," he said.

"But these men are your friends," said the Queen.

"Yes," agreed Macbeth. "But I did not risk my own life just to give my crown to Fleance."

Macbeth and the Queen made a plan. They decided to have a banquet and invite all of the leaders in the kingdom. "It will be a feast for the new King," said the Queen.

"I will invite Banquo and Fleance to this feast," said Macbeth. "But I will make sure that they never get to the castle alive!"

Macbeth hired three men to murder Banquo and Fleance. "You must not fail to kill them," Macbeth told the men.

The men smiled. "There are three of us and there are only two of them," said one of the men. "Banquo and Fleance will not be at your party. They will spend the night in a ditch!"

Sure enough, Banquo and Fleance were not at the party. Macbeth seemed happy again as he spoke to people. He liked it when they called him King, and when they wished him a long life.

But, suddenly, Macbeth saw a stranger in the doorway. It was one of the men that he had hired to kill Banquo and Fleance. Macbeth excused himself and went over to the man.

"I see blood on your face," said Macbeth. "Did you kill them?"

"Banquo's throat is cut from ear to ear," said the man.

"What about Fleance?" asked Macbeth. "Is he dead, too?"

The man looked down. "I am sorry to tell you that Fleance escaped," he said.

Macbeth was angry. But people were calling him, so he turned and went back to the party.

"King Macbeth!" called one of the guests. "Please, come and sit with us at our table."

Macbeth tried his best to smile. "My good fellows," he said. "I would gladly join you at your table, but there is not one empty chair to sit in!"

Part 6 Macbeth **59**

One of the men slapped his hand on a chair. "Sit here! There is one chair left, and we are saving it for you!" he said.

Macbeth looked at the man. Then he looked at the chair. Someone was sitting there! It was the ghost of Banquo! His head was half cut off and his white face was covered with blood!

Part 7

Macbeth and the Witches

When he saw the ghost of Banquo, Macbeth turned pale and began to tremble. Then he began to talk to the ghost. The Queen rushed over to Macbeth. "What's wrong with you?" she asked. "You are talking to an empty chair."

No one except Macbeth could see Banquo's ghost. When the ghost did not go away, Macbeth began to speak to it again.

Now, everyone in the room was staring at Macbeth. The Queen became afraid.

"Macbeth will let everyone know that he killed Duncan and Banquo," she said to herself. "I must get him away from here."

When the room became quiet, the Queen spoke. "Dear friends," she said. "As you can see, the King is ill. It is nothing to worry about. I have seen him with this illness in the past. He needs rest, that's all," said the Queen. "I thank you all for coming, but I must ask you to leave now." So all the guests left the castle.

Macbeth did not sleep well that night. In his dreams, he saw the ghosts of King Duncan and Banquo. And he thought that he saw Fleance wearing a king's crown.

The next morning, Macbeth told his wife that he was going to find the three witches. "I must know more about the future," he explained.

The witches had known that Macbeth would come back to them. They had worked all night getting ready for him. In the middle of their room was a large, black cauldron.

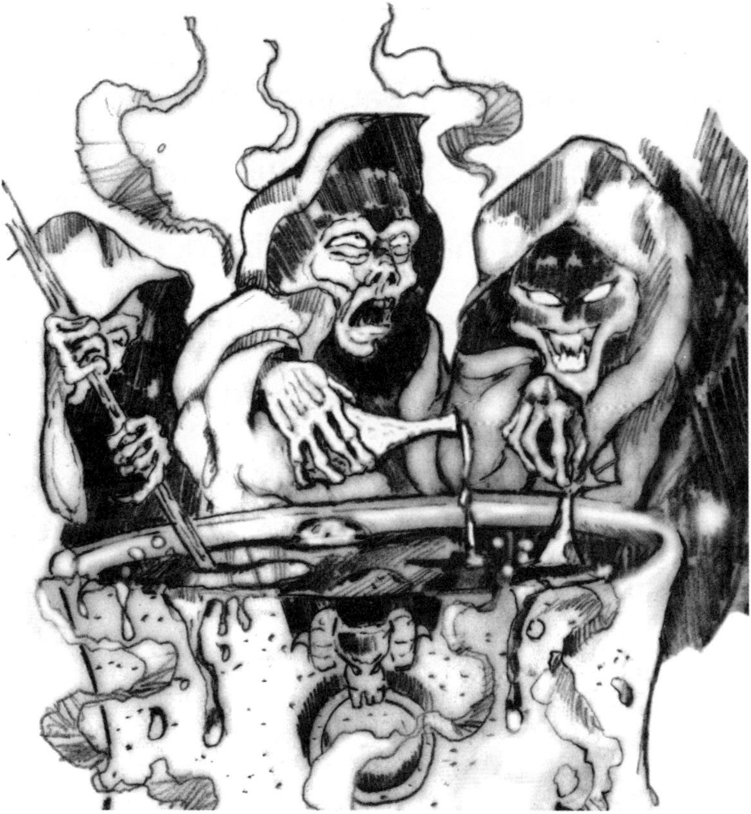

A cauldron is a big pot that is used for cooking. The witches had built a fire under the cauldron.

One witch dropped the toe of a frog and the wing of a bat into the cauldron. The second witch added the tongue of a dog and the leg of a lizard. The third witch dropped the finger of a dead child and the tooth of a wolf into the pot. Then all three witches sang:

"Trouble, trouble, toil and trouble;

Fire burn and cauldron bubble!

Cool it with a baboon's blood.

Then the charm is firm and good."

While the first witch was pouring the blood into the cauldron, Macbeth arrived in the doorway. The smoke and smell from the cauldron made him feel sick. "I must make them think that I am brave," he said to himself.

Macbeth took a deep breath and went inside. "I demand that you speak to me," he said.

"If you ask a question, we will answer it," said the second witch.

Macbeth watched as the witches poured more blood into the cauldron. Thick, dark smoke filled the air.

The witches began to sing again:

"Trouble, trouble, toil and trouble;

Fire burn and cauldron bubble!"

Part 8

Smoke and Blood

Macbeth stared into the smoke that was rising from the cauldron. Suddenly, he saw a head floating in the air! The head was wearing a helmet. It stared right back at Macbeth and then it spoke to him. "Macbeth, Macbeth, Macbeth," it said. "Beware of the Thane of Fife!" Macbeth knew that the Thane of Fife was General Macduff.

Then the head disappeared in the smoke. Next, Macbeth saw a small child floating in the air.

The child was covered with blood. "Macbeth, Macbeth, Macbeth," said the child. "Be brave and be bold, for no man can hurt you if he was born of a woman."

Macbeth smiled. "Then I do not need to be afraid of Macduff after all," he said to himself. "Certainly, he was born of a woman."

Macbeth looked back into the smoke. This time, a different child was floating there. This child was wearing a crown and holding the branch of a tree.

Macbeth listened as the child spoke. "No one shall ever defeat Macbeth until the forest at Birnam Wood moves to his castle at Dunsinane," said the child.

Macbeth felt happy. "No one can ever defeat me!" he said. "No man can hurt me if he was born of a woman. All men are born of women. And no army can defeat me until the forest at Birnam Wood moves to Dunsinane!" Macbeth laughed. "Who has ever heard of a forest moving anywhere?" he asked.

Macbeth looked at the witches. "I have one last question," he said. "Will Banquo ever have a son who will become King?" asked Macbeth.

"Do not ask any more questions!" said a witch.

"You must answer me!" cried Macbeth.

The witches turned and looked into the smoke. Macbeth looked also. He saw a row of eight kings floating in the air, and at the end of the row was the ghost of Banquo.

He was pointing at the other men and smiling, so Macbeth knew that these other men were Banquo's sons and grandsons and great-grandsons.

Then, suddenly, Macbeth was alone. The witches were gone. The cauldron was gone. Even the smoke was gone.

"I cannot worry about the future," Macbeth said to himself. "I must worry about today. I must murder Macduff, the Thane of Fife!"

When Macbeth returned to the royal castle, he asked his soldiers about Macduff. "General Macduff is on his way to England," said a soldier. "He is going to England to meet with Malcolm, King Duncan's son. Macduff plans to join his army with Malcolm's army."

"Go after him! Stop him! Kill him!" roared Macbeth. "And kill his family, too."

The King's soldiers left as fast as they could. They rode to Macduff's castle and broke down the door.

When they got inside, one of the soldiers yelled, "The King demands to see General Macduff, the Thane of Fife!"

Macduff's wife and son came into the room with the soldiers. "My husband is not here," said Lady Macduff.

"Then where will we find him?" asked the soldier.

"I will not tell you," she replied.

"Your husband is a traitor to King Macbeth," said the soldier.

Part 8   Macbeth   77

When Macduff's son heard this, he became angry. "How dare you call my father a traitor!" he cried. "You are a liar, sir!"

The soldiers drew their swords. They killed Lady Macduff and her son and all of her other children in the castle.

Part 9

The Forest Moves

General Macduff was now in England. He was meeting with Malcolm. Macduff and Malcolm were talking about Scotland. They were remembering the days when King Duncan had ruled the country.

"My father was a good king," said Malcolm.

"Macbeth is an evil king," said Macduff. "We must stop him."

Just then, a messenger came into the room. Macduff saw that it was his friend, Ross. Ross was upset.

"Do you have news for me, Ross?" asked Macduff.

"I have terrible news," said Ross. "Macbeth's soldiers have broken down the door of your castle. They have killed your wife and children."

Macduff felt as if he had been stabbed. Macbeth had killed King Duncan and the King's guards! He had killed Banquo and he had tried to kill Banquo's son, Fleance! And now he had killed Macduff's wife and children.

"We shall put our armies together," Macduff said to Malcolm. "And we shall crush Macbeth on the hills of Dunsinane!"

While these two large armies marched toward Scotland, Macbeth took his small army to the castle at Dunsinane. Macbeth's army was small because everyone hated him now, and most of his soldiers refused to fight for him.

But Macbeth did not seem to care. "I cannot be defeated!" he said. "Every man was born of a woman. And everyone knows that a forest cannot move. Let Macduff and Malcolm try to stop me," said Macbeth. "I will kill them all."

Lady Macbeth waited inside the castle. She had always been an evil woman. But when she heard the news about Macduff's dead wife and children, she lost her mind. She began to sleepwalk in the middle of the night and talk to herself.

She complained to her servant that she could smell blood. She stared at her hands and rubbed them together all day long, as if she could not get her hands clean.

"There is a spot on my hand, and I cannot get it off," said Lady Macbeth to a servant.

"Your hands are as clean as the snow," replied the servant.

But Lady Macbeth did not seem to hear. She kept rubbing her hands and saying, "Out, damned spot! Out, I say!"

Part 9   Macbeth   85

One night, Lady Macbeth went to bed alone and killed herself.

King Macbeth was standing on the top of a hill near the castle. He was waiting for Macduff and Malcolm and their armies. A servant brought him the news that his wife was dead. Macbeth's face turned pale, and for a few minutes he could not speak. "Why should I keep on living?" he asked. "Life has no meaning."

Suddenly, a soldier called to Macbeth. "Look, there!" he cried. The soldier was pointing at the forest. "The trees are moving!" he said.

Macbeth could not believe his eyes. In the moonlight, he saw a whole forest of trees moving slowly toward the castle at Dunsinane! "How can this be?" he asked himself.

Macduff and Malcolm's soldiers were marching toward the castle.

The generals had said to their soldiers, "Cut down a small tree and carry it with you. Hide behind the tree so that no one can see you."

Macbeth could not see the soldiers, but he could see the trees moving closer and closer to Dunsinane. "I am still not afraid," he said. "Show me a man who was not born of a woman. That is the only man who can hurt me. And there is no such man."

Part 10

Macbeth Meets the Thane of Fife

Macduff and Malcolm and their soldiers were near the castle now. "Remember," Macduff told the soldiers. "Macbeth is mine to kill."

When the fighting began, many of Macbeth's own soldiers joined Macduff and Malcolm's army.

Macbeth sat on his horse like a giant. He had always been brave in battle, but now he thought that no man could hurt him.

Suddenly, Macbeth came face to face with Macduff. The King remembered the warning from the witches' cauldron. 'Beware of the Thane of Fife!' Now Macduff, the Thane of Fife, was sitting on his horse, right in front of Macbeth!

"You must stay away from me!" called Macbeth. "My sword is already stained with the blood of your family."

"I will let my sword speak for me," said Macduff.

"Tell me this," said Macbeth. "How were you born? Were you born of a woman?" he asked.

Macduff raised his sword into the air. "I never knew my mother," he replied. "She died while I was being born. The doctor ripped me from her belly!"

Macbeth groaned. Here was the Thane of Fife. Beware of the Thane of Fife. Here was the man who had made the trees move. Here was the man who had not been born of a woman.

The sword that Macbeth was holding felt heavy. He thought that he could smell blood in the air. "It is my blood now," Macbeth told himself.

There was a loud pounding of a horse's hooves. Macduff screamed out the names of his wife and children. He charged at Macbeth while the soldiers watched in fear. And, with one mighty swing of his sword, he cut off Macbeth's head.

Then Macduff turned his horse around and rode slowly back to the headless body. Macduff was still holding his sword as he got down from his horse. He picked up Macbeth's head by the hair and he stuck it onto the end of his sword. Then Macduff carried the sword to Malcolm.

"Here is the head of Macbeth," he shouted. "We are free!"

Part 10 Macbeth **95**

Malcolm held the sword up high so that all of the soldiers could see that Macbeth was dead at last.

A cheer went up from the soldiers. "All hail King Malcolm!" they cried. "All hail, Malcolm, the new King of Scotland!"

The End

A Note from the Start-to-Finish Editors

You will notice that Start-to-Finish Books look different from other high-low readers and chapter books. The text layout of this book coordinates with the other media components (CD and audiocassette) of the Start-to-Finish series.

The text in the book matches, line-for-line and page-for-page, the text shown on the computer screen, enabling readers to follow along easily in the book. Each page ends in a complete sentence so that the student can either practice the page (repeat reading) or turn the page to continue with the story. If the next sentence cannot fit on the page in its entirety, it has been shifted to the next page. For this reason, the sentence at the top of a page may not be indented, signaling that it is part of the paragraph from the preceding page.

Words are not hyphenated at the ends of lines. This sometimes creates extra space at the end of a line, but eliminates confusion for the struggling reader.